PEOPLE MATHS: HIDDEN DEPTHS

PEOPLE MATHS
HIDDEN DEPTHS

Alan Bloomfield & Bob Vertes

ATM

Published by the Association of Teachers of Mathematics, 2005

Design: DCG Design, Cambridge

Contents

Alan Bloomfield

Bob Vertes

Alan is Suffolk born and bred, and an Ipswich Town addict despite working in Gloucestershire. He manages as a job, teaches as a vocation and loves doing maths as it's part of him. He has run People Maths sessions in Africa, Asia, Europe and America and is hoping for an invitation to New Zealand sometime.

Bob was born in Budapest, Hungary, where he first saw Manchester United; ended his first day at infant school by declaring he wanted to be a teacher and here he is today, with over 30 years in schools, in teacher education, and with the Open University. He loves problem solving, puzzles and games as approaches to learning maths – and those (awful) jokes!

They hope that all the people they have met in a combined 70 years of teaching will buy this book! – and that some will send them ideas for the next one.

Introduction

'People mathematics' uses people to form the moving pieces of a mathematical activity, be it a puzzle, a sum, a diagram or a demonstration. Often the activity has a definite end-point, which everyone can recognise. There may be many methods of reaching an end-point, but some will be more efficient than others. For example a puzzle may be solved in a minimum number of moves.

These activities have the potential for rich mathematical exploration and investigation. Often they could have been modelled by using counters or cubes and certainly many could be completed in a solitary fashion using pencil & paper or a computer. What makes them worthy of the title 'People Maths' is the fact they can all be initiated by using people in place of the other kinds of resources, thereby encouraging pupil-pupil discussion. Although pupil-teacher discussion can also take place, with people maths the emphasis is heavily on discussion within the group taking part. Indeed it is the need for such discussion to take place that makes it so worthwhile

to use People Maths in Primary and Secondary classrooms.

The view one takes of any mathematical experience depends to a large extent on what view one has of the nature of mathematics and of learning mathematics. Some may see mathematics in terms of a body of knowledge to be acquired by appropriate teacher-led experiences. They would find it harder to justify using time on any activity that did not lead directly to an increase in a pupil's understanding of some part of this body of recognised knowledge. Such a content-driven approach may seem to exclude People Maths as an acceptable activity. However, by providing experiences which illustrate a real need for say, algebraic notation, the motivation to obtain access to the content of mathematics is increased. There are also activities in this book that seek directly to help pupils to understand or to consolidate understanding of some particular mathematical topic. Using pupils to shift along a number line may, for example, provide a concrete representation of the addition and

subtraction of integers. The demonstration of the sum of an infinite series using people is another such example, as might be our approach in this book to teaching and learning about loci.

Many mathematicians reject a narrow view of the subject and see mathematics as a field for investigation, where you can choose your own questions to ask and invent your own structures to manipulate and communicate. There are standard processes of enquiry and tricks of the trade, which can help, but the student owns the mathematics. This view of the nature of mathematics places a great value on autonomy and creativity. The activities within this book are planned with this role in mind.

Some themes we hope you will spot in this book are Puzzles, Problems, Proof, and Participation. The (Mathematics in the) National Curriculum (document) for England – of which we have deliberately avoided any mention elsewhere in this book – prefaces all content listing in the *Programmes of Study* with the phrase 'pupils should be taught . . .' For this book our philosophy is that 'pupils should be actively involved in learning . . .'; and while we expect that pupils will achieve success in learning mathematics via these activities, we have deliberately avoided measuring such learning via Attainment Targets and levels.

No book on People Maths can get away without mentioning the role of the Association of Teachers of Mathematics (ATM). Both of us are certain that we owe an enormous amount to ATM for promoting active mathematics through its annual Easter conference, its branch meetings and its publications. Our friends and colleagues at ATM have encouraged us to write this book and we are grateful for the gentle reminders and positive feedback we have had from Heather McLeay and others on the ATM publications committee.

We also have a debt to countless other mathematicians, teachers and authors for their ideas. Although we would lay claim to having invented many of the activities we are not going to be foolish enough to identify which. It is likely that someone else got there first; perhaps by several hundred years.

As an example there are plenty of references to Activity 25 (FROGS) in the journals of the ATM (for example, *Micromath* Volume 1/Number 2, Autumn 1985, contains articles on the investigation) and we make no claim here to originality. However activities in these pages are often much older than even the first volume of *Micromath*. This particular game dates from the nineteenth century, where the pieces were then cardboard frogs. Edouard Lucas described the puzzle and its solution in 1883. A number of illustrations of the 'Jeu Des Grenouilles' in its various forms are to be found in *Puzzles Old and New* by Slocum and Botermans.

We are very grateful to colleagues and students at our respective institutions, the University of Gloucestershire, and St Mary's College in Twickenham, London. Their support and encouragement have been significant factors in our successful development of many of these activities, and in writing this book. In 2001 St Mary's College awarded Bob the St Henry Walpole Award for Excellence in Teaching, following external recognition by Ofsted and an internal competition. This annual award includes a significant monetary prize, which assisted greatly in developing and trialling many of the activities in this book. These approaches also contributed to Bob being shortlisted in 2003 for the ILTHE National Teaching Fellowship scheme. Bob would like to acknowledge the support given by St Mary's College and its staff, which contributed to the achievement of these honours.

David Cutting, DCG Design, has contributed helpful comments on text and presentation beyond all expectations. We would like to thank him. We are also grateful as ever to Jill and Marilyn respectively for their tolerance in coping with us and caring for us, when we were under pressure. We would like to acknowledge the contribution to this book by many others. We apologise for not being able to name them but know that they would share our enthusiasm. We hope that the activities will be of value to teachers and learners of mathematics in future years.

Alan Bloomfield and **Bob Vertes**
March 2005

1 Why use People Maths?

Part of the motivation for this book is the realisation for both of us that learning, and later teaching, mathematics was sometimes insufficiently exciting and enjoyable without a sense of actively doing mathematics. In many of these activities we are exploring the activity, and having some fun, but behind it is the realisation that we are also exploring some mathematics. The pleasure of participating in the activity motivates the further exploration of the mathematics behind it. It will be important, if these activities are tried by readers, that time is given to such follow up of the activity. Games playing is fine and worthy of use of spare time, but we feel these are purposeful ways of initiating or developing the learning of mathematics. Hence the title includes *Hidden Depths* and not just *People Maths*.

Our activities are all designed so as not to criticise or humiliate people by forcing them to make mistakes in public. A former UK Minister of Education, saying that $7 \times 8 = 54$ on national radio, was vilified. He has at least a little of our sympathy; mistakes occur when people are pressurised publicly. It's just unfortunate he was there to talk about the need for numeracy tests for teachers. We hope our activities will encourage people doing maths to be willing to take risks, without feeling threatened by the fear of error or failure. We think the collaborative approach we recommend will encourage people to suggest solutions to activities. We know that confidence (whether lack of it, building it, or retaining it) is a major factor in the learning of mathematics.

We believe that collaboration in learning is vital and that kinæsthetic approaches to learning can offer real opportunities for learners. These approaches have historically been under-represented in the mathematics classroom.

Our experience of using people mathematics over a range of ages of participants from 5 to 75, in schools, clubs, conferences, teacher training courses and Open University sessions, tells us it works. We know its value and we will try to exemplify this in the following descriptions.

Description One

Bob Vertes has been running a Mathematics afternoon at Collingwood College in Camberley, Surrey, an 11–18 mixed school, for some years, towards the end of the summer term. About 120 Y7 pupils and a number of Y6 (future Collingwood) pupils from 3 or 4 feeder primary schools are gathered in a school hall. Their maths teachers, some parents, and a number of Bob's future PGCE mathematics trainees are the managers of a group of pupils for each activity. We normally have time for two or three of the activities in an afternoon, with a brief public introduction to each activity, then time to carry it out, and finally to share and record some results. There would then be an opportunity to review the whole afternoon before it ends. Popular activities on these occasions include SQUARE PAIRS, NUMBER SANDWICHES, ROBAPS, and TRIPLES (Activities 32, 35, 7 and 33). It has been interesting to hear teachers unused to these approaches describing how some pupils have unexpectedly flourished; some who were quiet in class, some who were a behaviour management problem, seem to come alive, become focused and participate enthusiastically. We also retain the goodwill of those more familiar with, and perhaps more comfortable with, more traditional approaches. The pupils also seem to have a great time but their work is really fruitful when in class over the next few days the activities are followed up.

The primary school staff and parents have always been generous with their praise. One can always predict a few "I wish I had been taught maths this way", but they and the staff from the schools so often ask – "where can we find out about more of these activities?" Equally interesting in these sessions is the reaction of the future teachers, the trainees: they have the chance not only to practise their classroom management skills, but also to widen their eyes to a greater range of strategies for teaching and learning maths.

Description Two

One important benefit of this kinæsthetic approach to mathematics, warming the heart of someone like Bob for whom English is not his first language, is the comfort and enthusiasm to participate of those whose linguistic confidence and skills may not yet be strong. By providing an opportunity to work kinæstheti-

cally one gives so many additional signals to aid understanding.

These activities are regularly used, for example, in the London Borough of Hounslow Maths days for gifted and talented pupils, and also as part of the government's *Aim Higher* initiatives. The way Hounslow uses them is to have pupils working in mixed teams for the day to enable them to work with pupils from other schools. The teams participate in a circus of 4 or 5 activities through the course of a day, taking about 45 minutes to an hour per activity. ROBAPS and SQUARE PAIRS (Activities 7, 32) again have proved successful activities at these occasions. About 15-20 (usually Y7, Y8, or Y9) pupils are normally sent from each school to the host location, about 6 schools at a time, whose commitment must be that at least one maths teacher accompanies the group. It helps if they have previously attended one of the previous sessions, otherwise the instinct of the teachers can be to make the sessions and activities too teacher-led and excessively results-focused. This is not helpful to the participants!

The discussion parts are the most fruitful, and ideally the participants take their work back to school where others can share the approaches and some of the ideas can be followed up, whether in class or in a Maths club. It has been helpful that prospective and

sometimes current or recent PGCE trainees (who may have been introduced to these approaches in their course) also attend to assist. Pupil reactions have been really positive, especially for some pupils who have extended some of the activities, using variations of the rules, to explore what differences in results occur. Some pupils thrive on self-imposed competition; others respond particularly well to the collaborative learning involved.

Another benefit is an increase in pupils' confidence and leadership skills when various members of a class are given the manager role, e.g. for a number of these activities to be in charge of a group of say 6 peers – see THE CLICK GAME, or PAIR PRODUCT SUMS (Activities 14, 34).

Description Three

The following two descriptions describe experiences Alan has had of using People Maths with pupils in Gloucestershire.

I decided that I would use three one-hour sessions with a group of thirty 13-year-old pupils in a local comprehensive school to encourage cooperative group work in mathematics. I wanted the pupils to spend a considerable amount of time on one extended task and felt that GRASSHOPPERS (Activity 5) would be suitably accessible and yet contain plenty of hidden depth for further investigation. Having put all tables to the side of the room the pupils were sat in a large circle. I then asked for 4 volunteers to try to solve a puzzle and explained the rules for GRASSHOP-PERS. Working in the centre of the circle the 4 volunteers succeeded but not in the minimum number of moves. The class then split into groups of 5 to try the puzzle first with 4 and then 5 people. When the groups had had an opportunity to succeed, we discussed what had happened and what sort of questions they could ask. The groups then looked at GRASSHOP-PERS with 6, 7, 8 people splitting up groups themselves to get the right number of participants. Naturally there was some competition between groups to reduce the number of moves for these cases. Pupils then started to record their moves in order to check themselves and to explain to others when challenged.

The next session involved a recap of what had happened the previous week, followed by pupils working in self-selected small groups on extensions to the basic puzzle. Each group was to contribute part of their findings to a display explaining what the class had done. These results and diagrams were to be the joint work of each small group. During this session, apart from the recap at the beginning, pupils used counters or small pieces of paper rather than still investigating the game as a people game. The last session was spent in producing this record of what had occurred.

Description Four

This was a single session with a group of 22 Y8 Secondary pupils. These pupils were in the 'bottom' set for mathematics, but were excellent at working cooperatively in small groups. When team-teaching with their usual teacher for the first time I was immediately impressed at the extent to which they would come together in small groups to plan their strategy for solving a problem. In this case it was "Guess the (whole) number. I'm thinking of between 1 and 100".

The People Maths session lasted one hour. Having arranged the children into groups of 5 and 6 we played several games of SORTING (see Activity 24) including turning the question round "Which group can give me a name with a multiplication score of 7?" Their cries of "You can't do that" and "It's prime" were followed by first name J and a surname of 7 letters.

The second half of the session centred on STEPPING STONES (Activity 3). I gave the briefest of descriptions for the six-person game with 5 stones and then sent the pupils off into groups to plan their solution together, with the aim of effecting a crossing in the fewest possible moves. The last few minutes were then spent with each group demonstrating their method of crossing. No group made the crossing in the minimum number of 21, but all the groups managed a crossing in around 24 moves. Incidentally few groups obtain a solution in 21 moves; 23 is usually the best achieved in a short time.

What had happened? All the pupils had worked enthusiastically for the whole session. In the sorting games they had compared answers and checked each other's answers. It was the group's responsibility to get things right, not the individual's. There was no written work, but plenty of challenge in the STEPPING STONES. Most importantly one pupil who was normally very quiet and hardly spoke became a very active and fully integrated member of her group. That on its own made the session worthwhile.

Additional Notes on some of the Activities

Other areas of the curriculum can be taught using People Maths, catering more appropriately especially for those pupils whose preferred learning styles are kinæsthetic, visual and practical.

An example might be to convince that the sum of the external angles of a polygon is 360°. A number of points are marked on the classroom floor, say 5. A pupil stands by one such point facing towards the next. She moves to that point, turns to face the next, and the angle she has turned through is marked. This continues until she returns to her starting point, at which time she has still to turn to face the original direction.

It will be clear that the angles marked are the external angles of the polygon, and it will only be at the last that she again faces the same direction, i.e. will have made a complete turn, i.e. 360°. Seymour Papert, the thinker behind Logo, describes this as the Total Turtle Turn Theorem, sometimes abbreviated to T^4.

Aha! moments and the Eureka strategy

When working in a large group, in class or otherwise, it can be helpful to discourage the calling out of guesses or even answers to the whole group. One of the benefits of these investigative approaches is the pleasure learners feel with the *Aha!* moment, when 'the penny drops', 'the light switches on'. In order to maximise the opportunity for the majority of a group to gain this effect, it can be helpful to encourage those thinking they know an answer not to call it out but to indicate it by saying "Eureka". This also gives the manager of learning the chance to gauge how many of a

class are at an appropriate point for whole-group discussion or review; we are aware as experienced teacher educators how trainee teachers are especially prone to assuming that if one person in a class gives the right answer, the whole class could.

Questioning

Although it is no doubt a well understood approach for many of our readers, we want to reinforce the idea that questioning, even if sometimes it is with leading or cueing questions, is more fruitful to encourage active participation, thinking and learning than excessive teacher-led styles. In many cases it is the process that we wish to foster, rather than the product. It does not matter if the teacher does not always know the answer to every question pupils may ask. It would suggest that the questions coming forward were all too directed and controlled.

Indeed the most effective learning will come if the teacher gives the pupils the freedom to ask and answer their own questions, give their explanations, make the rules, challenge each other to explain more clearly, to convince and to prove.

Recording

Many of the activities here are accompanied by a recommendation that participants record their results, noting intermediate steps as well as final answers. Much of the benefit of some of the activities will be missed if this advice to record is neglected! Pupils will also gain from having to devise their own appropriate forms of recording.

The Activities **2**

1 6-SQUARE PROBLEM

Resources needed

5 people

6 chairs

cards: 1 to 5 or labels

It is also helpful to have people to help record moves

Seat X is empty in both cases.

Task

Move the people from their starting positions in diagram A so that they return to the right order as in diagram B.

Rules

Moves are 'horizontal' or 'vertical' (as in the plastic sliding piece puzzles).

Questions

1 Can it be done?

2 How many moves?

3 Strategies?

Variations

Try different starting positions, more chairs and more people.

Hints and Hidden Depths

Try working out from which starting positions it is possible to get back to the final order as in diagram B above.

Start with swapping pairs of numbers. This problem is closely related to Sam Loyd's 15 puzzle and other sliding piece puzzles.

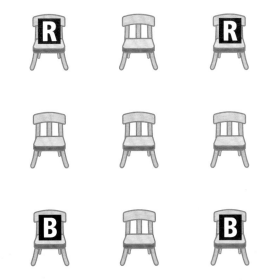

Resources needed

4 people: two labelled red and two labelled black

9 chairs

Task

Interchange Red and Black by moving one at a time.

Rules

The four players work together to solve the problem, and can move in any order. Moves are those of a knight in chess (2 places in one direction and one at right angles or vice versa).

Questions

Can it be done?

How many moves?

Strategies?

Variations

Try a larger array and more knights . . .

Different moves, for example 1-3 (1 across and 3 down) rather than 1-2.

Hints and Hidden Depths

As with many of the puzzles some form of recording is important. For example in this case using coordinates for the boxes may be best.

Resources needed

6 people in two groups of three

5 hoops to represent stepping stones

Task

Interchange the two groups by moving one person at a time. The six people can move in any order, collaborating to solve the problem.

Rules

There are two kinds of moves:

1 Steps (move onto an empty adjacent stone).

2 Swings (swing someone around you to land on an empty stone).

Questions

How many moves?

Strategies for getting there in the fewest moves?

Variations

Fewer stones and fewer people.

More stones and more people.

Change the rules.

Hints and Hidden Depths

It can help to record the number of steps, the number of swings and the total number of moves. It is worthwhile looking for a pattern in the moves which lead to an optimal solution.

See also 'FROGS' (Activity 25).

Rule 2

Resources needed

6 people

7 chairs

For variations, one more chair than the number of people

Task

Working as a team, the task is to get everyone to sit down on an empty chair according to the rule below. You begin with everybody standing.

Rule

You must find an empty chair then count on three places clockwise to find another empty chair. Then you sit down. If this isn't possible then you all need to start again.

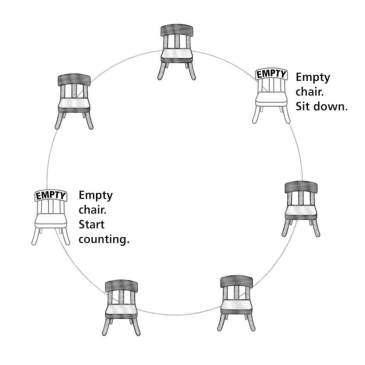

EMPTY Empty chair. Sit down.

EMPTY Empty chair. Start counting.

Questions

Can it be done?

How many moves?

Strategies?

Variations

Try different numbers of people.

Try counting on for a different number of chairs instead of three clockwise.

Hints and Hidden Depths

This is a variation of an ancient Babylonian game and nothing to do with 'musical chairs' which would have one less chair than the number of people!

See Phil Dodd, *Mathematics From Around The World*.

5 GRASSHOPPERS

Resources needed

7 people

8 chairs

Cards 1 to 7 (or labels)

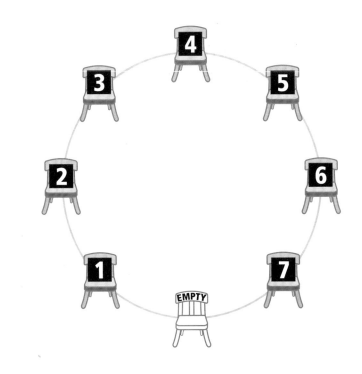

Task

Begin with everyone sitting down. Each person wears a number card or label. Reverse the order in which they sit but end with the empty chair in the same place as at the start.

Rules

Grasshoppers may slide to an adjoining empty chair or leap across one person to the empty chair.

Questions

Can it be done?

How many moves?

Strategies?

Variations

More people, more empty chairs, fitter grasshoppers can jump further.

Evens anticlockwise and odds clockwise.

Hints and Hidden Depths

As in many of the movement games/puzzles, the easiest way to record a solution is to note the number of the person who moves at any particular time. So for four people a solution might be 1, 4, 3, 2, 3, 1; a total of six moves.

Investigate the connection between the number of moves and the number of people. The algebraic formula for the number of moves is not as straightforward as it is for 'FROGS' (Activity 25).

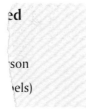

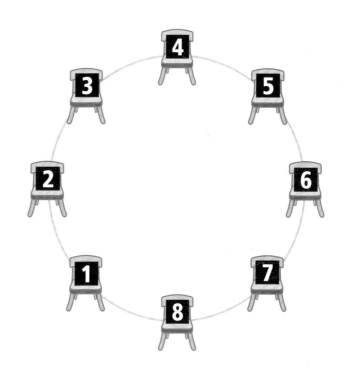

Task

Reverse the order of seating.

Rules

Any two people swap places.

Questions

Can it be done?

How many moves?

Strategies?

Variations

More people.

Rules for swaps e.g. only adjacent pairs can swap, or only those with one person between them.

Hints and Hidden Depths

What is the best strategy for the minimum number of pair swaps?

Is there a rule for the minimum number of swaps for a given number of people?

How does this compare with GRASSHOPPERS (Activity 5)?

How does this compare with ROBAPS (Activity 7)?

7 ROBAPS

Resources needed

6 people

Cards numbered 1 to 6

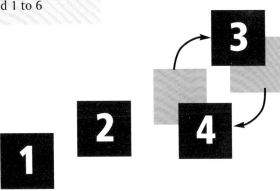

Task

'**R**everse **O**rder **B**y **A**djacent **P**air Swaps' – acronym is ROBAPS.

Each person is labelled.

People line up in numerical sequence.

People change places in adjacent pairs.

The number of such swaps required to finish in reverse order is counted.

Questions

How many moves (of pairs) are required?

Does the order of moves affect the number to reverse the numbers?

Is there a 'best' order of moves?

Variations

Try with different numbers of people.

Try having a rule of swapping only pairs with one person between them.

Try rule of 'at least one person between'.

Hints and Hidden Depths

Investigate connections between the number of people and the number of moves.

Explore connections with triangular numbers.

How does this compare with TWIN TURNS (Activity 8)?

20

Resources needed

6 people (3 male & 3 female or colour coded in some way into two groups of three)

8 chairs

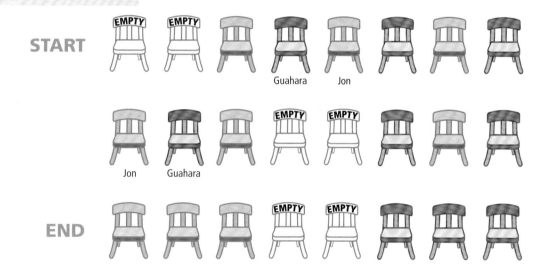

START

Guahara   Jon

Jon   Guahara

END

Task

The group starts sitting as in diagram with empty chairs at one end and people sitting alternately in their two groups.

The object is to separate the two groups with the two empty chairs between them.

Rules

Two people who are occupying adjoining chairs stand up. They then sit down in the two chairs which were empty, but first they change sides.

Suppose Guahara and Jon move. If Guahara was originally on Jon's left then after moving Guahara will be on Jon's right hand side.

Variations

Try different numbers of people, e.g. with four in each group rather than three, for example.

Try moving three people rather than two, with the outside pair swapping places before sitting down in three empty chairs.

Questions

What is the minimum number of twin turns to separate the groups?

Hints and Hidden Depths

Investigate connections between the number of people and the number of moves.

Explore connections with triangular numbers.

9 PLAIN HUNT ON SIX

Resources needed

6 people

6 chairs

Change A

Change B

Task

Each person chooses a sound to make; it could be calling out the number 1,2,3,4,5,6 if inspiration fails.

Then change places as in change A. Swap in pairs. Make the sounds in the new order 2, 1, 4, 3, 6, 5.

Now execute change B (See how the end people sit still while the others change in pairs).

Make the sounds in the new order.

Carry out with change A followed by change B until it seems right to stop.

Questions

What happens?

How many changes?

Do you get all possible permutations?

Variations

Plain Hunt without changing places just by order of the sound.

Silent plain hunt (by raising arm no sound).

Other changes.

Hints and Hidden Depths

Try more people, other changes, card shuffles, riffle shuffles.

Go bell-ringing.

Resources needed

6-10 people

Labels or cards numbered from 1-10 can help keep track of movements

Original order

1 2 3 4 5 6

After 1 round, a 4 cut

5 6 1 2 3 4

Task

Each person is labelled and the group line up in numerical order. It is best to record this list e.g. on the board.

Then the group choose a cut. The example shown uses a cut of 4.

This means the first 4 in line move to the back to form a new list, resulting as in change shown.

Each completed new row counts as one round. It is best to record each new row, to help with pattern spotting.

Count the number of rounds required until you reach the original line-up. You must use the same cut each time. In this example a cut of 4.

Try different numbers of people in the line-up but explore all the cuts possible for each.

Questions

What happens?

How many rounds are needed?

Do any people only move to a limited number of positions?

Which 'cut numbers', for a given number of people in line, lead to every number taking a turn being at the head of the line-up?

Which 'cut numbers', for a given number of people in line, lead to faster than expected returns to the original line-up?

Variations

Try taking every second person to go to the back. This time it will be really important to keep track of the position numbers.

Hints and Hidden Depths

Look carefully at cut numbers which are factors of the starting number of people; look also at when these two numbers are co-prime.

11 BACK-FRONT SHUFFLES

Resources needed

6-10 people

Cards 1-10 (or labels)

Front   Back

Original order 1 2 3 4 5 6

After 1 round 6 1 5 2 4 3

Task

Each person is labelled and the group lines up in numerical order. It is best to record this list e.g. on a board.

Then the people change places to form a new order, moving in turn: first the person at the back starts a new line from the front. Then the person at the front moves, etc., resulting in the new row 615243.

Each completed new row counts as one round. It is best to record each new row, to help with pattern spotting.

Count the number of rounds required until you reach the original line-up.

Is it possible to predict, for a given number of people in line, how many rounds it will take to 'return'?

Questions

What happens?

How many changes?

Do any people stay in the same position?

Do any people only move to a limited number of positions?

What is noticeable about the numbers in the line-up just before we return to the original line-up?

Variations

Try different numbers of people in the line-up – recommend trying 6, 5, 8 (this gives a nice surprise).

Try front-back shuffles. How do they relate to back-front shuffles?

Hints and Hidden Depths

Look carefully at odd and even number of people and the number of rounds it takes to get back to the start order. What happens with 'power of 2' people?

See Chapter 3.

Resources needed

6 people

Cards 1 to 6

Chairs for each person can assist

A 'caller' or manager is useful

Starting order, for example

After first step

At the end of first sweep

Task

Each person is labelled, and the people arrange themselves in a random order.

A Caller manages the process of rearrangement into a correct sequence using 'bubble sort'.

(The first two are compared. If the first is bigger than the second then they swap.

The second and third, third and fourth etc are compared, swapping or staying still.

Once the end of the line is reached another sweep, starting at the front, is carried out.)

Questions

What is the number of steps required to complete a sort?

Are there other more (or less) efficient sorting mechanisms?

Variations

Try other sorting processes.

Try other numbers of people.

Hints and Hidden Depths

This is a technique studied on Decision Maths AS/A2 level courses.

Resources needed

2 teams of equal numbers of people

Lab stools or chairs or a grid of square tiles outside

Task

Teams take alternate turns to move one person one space forward or, if blocked by an opponent, they can move one space backwards.

The winning team is the one that forces its opponents back to their starting positions.

It is easy to work out who wins here, so change the rules when people have worked out what is happening.

Advanced rules

Each team can move either 1 or 2 spaces forward or backward, choosing which each turn.

Questions

Which team is going to win?

What happens if you change the grid?

Variations

Try different numbers of people.

Try a different number of tiles to count on.

Hints and Hidden Depths

Many animals will pretend to attack and then retreat cautiously after a suitable display of aggression. Once you have played the game the name makes sense. The trick is to force your opponent to retreat.

Resources needed

6 people to a team

Perhaps a 'caller' or 'manager' per team – helpful to have them primed with rules in advance

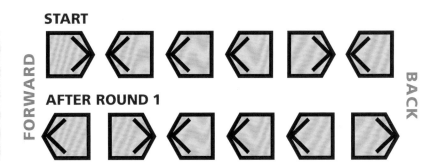

START

FORWARD

AFTER ROUND 1

BACK

Task

The teams line up. Each person in the team chooses to face 'forward' or 'back'. A click or sound is made, e.g. by 'caller'.

If, and only if, you are facing a person, you turn round through 180°. If there are any pairs who move, it counts as a successful round, and scores 1.

Carry out as many rounds as possible until it is impossible to move on any round. No addition to the team score can be made.

The 'caller' needs to ensure that only facing pairs move.

Questions

What scores are possible?

What initial arrangements give the maximum score?

How many different maximum scoring initial arrangements are there?

Can you get all the possible scores from 0 to the maximum?

Variations

Try scoring 1 point for each pair that move, and ask the same questions.

Hints and Hidden Depths

Try fewer/more people, and try to predict the maximum score for a class (30?) in line. Describe possible initial line arrangement(s) to obtain this maximum.

If the initial line-up is in a circle, what scores are possible and by what initial arrangements?

15 HANDS ON

Resources needed

Teams of people (6 per team is manageable as a starter)

Labels numbered 1- 6

Task

Your team members have to make as may links as possible by placing their hands on the shoulders of each other.

A link is, for example, when person 2 places a hand on the shoulder of person 5 and person 3 also places a hand on the shoulder of person 5: $2+3 = 5$.

What is the largest number of links you can make with six people?

Variations

What happens with other rules for making a link?

How might you show $5 - 3 = 2$?

The idea to try subtraction came from a group of first year B.Ed. Primary students at the University of Gloucestershire.

Questions

Try different numbers of people.

Is there a general rule here?

Hints and Hidden Depths

See the game 'KNOTS' (Activity 16)

Resources needed

Lots of people

A manager, or two

Tasks

People stand (roughly) in a circle.

A manager asks them first to close their eyes. They are asked to raise their hands to chest level or above.

People are then asked to move slowly forward until each of their hands has met with the hand of someone else. Each hand should grasp the hand it meets. Once grasped, they should not let go.

The manager(s) ensure that everyone has each hand linked to another person's hand.

Once that is done, people open their eyes.

The task is to unravel this giant group. People are not allowed to let go of the hand being held. Managers can help guide people in stepping over or under arms and legs, for example, or through 'hoops'.

Questions

What happens?

What shapes are created by the people's linked final positions?

When can one assume that further unknotting is impossible?

When are single or double loops formed?

Hints and Hidden Depths

Explore the theory of Knots. This activity can also be a nice starting point or follow-up to a study of Moebius strips.

17 STRING GAME

Resources needed

Teams of equal numbers of people (again 6 is a good starting point)

Labels numbered 1 to 6

Long enough piece of string or washing line

Lots of clothes pegs

Task

Teams stand in a circle in order.

A string passes from person 1 so that everyone is visited once and the string ends back at person 1. For example it might go as follows:

$$1 - 3 - 6 - 5 - 2 - 4 - 1$$

Pegs are then placed on each piece of string connecting two people. The number of pegs used is the difference between the two numbers.

So in this example 2, 3, 1, 3, 2 and 3 pegs are used on the various sections of string. A total of 14 pegs.

Questions

By using different orders for connecting people together:

What is the smallest total number of pegs?

What is the largest total number of pegs?

What totals can you find? Are there any totals you can't find?

Hints and Hidden Depths

The interesting task here is to prove why your totals are the largest and smallest.

An algebraic approach here may not be the best and thinking visually might just provide the key.

See Chapter 3.

Resources needed

People and space to operate . . . a hall is better than a small crowded room

Cones or small markers are useful

Questions

What happens in the long run?

How does this show that $\frac{1}{2} + \frac{1}{4} + \ldots = 1$?

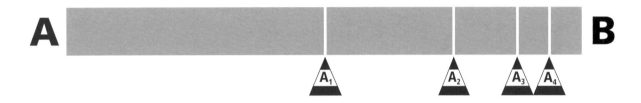

Demonstration

Person A stands at the end of the hall and moves towards person B at the other end, in stages. At each point A puts down a marker cone. Initially A goes halfway to B (A_1) and then half the remaining distance (A_2) and then carries on to A_3, which is a further 1/8 of the total towards B.

Variations

How can you use 3 people moving to show that:
$\frac{1}{4} + \frac{1}{16} + \frac{1}{64} \ldots = \frac{1}{3}$?

How can you use 2 people moving to show that:
$\frac{1}{3} + \frac{1}{9} + \frac{1}{27} \ldots = \frac{1}{2}$?

See diagram below for an idea.

Hints and Hidden Depths

Taken together these cases show an example of what we would term a people proof, although the full discussion about the use of the term 'proof' is outside the scope of this book.

We will settle for the term 'demonstration' here.

See Chapter 3.

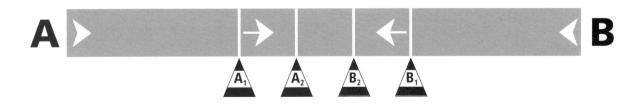

Resources needed

Two cones or cans as markers (it's easier if you can distinguish them by colour or by a large label)

Lots of people

Warm-up

People have to stand in positions satisfying the given rule.

Suppose the two cones are placed some distance apart (suggest 5m or so but it depends how much space you have).

Kelly is asked to stand so as to be exactly the same distance from the two cones.

Pete then has to stand somewhere new to satisfy this rule, then so do at least 6 others, in turn.

People will be standing on a straight line, the perpendicular bisector of the segment between the cones.

Task

If the two cones are A (black) and B (red), get people to stand in positions where they are twice as far from A as they are from B. So if P is the movable point obeying this rule, AP = 2BP.

What is the path now?

Questions

What is the shape?

How might you prove your conjecture?

Variations

AP = 3 PB

AP = 4 PB

AP = 1/2 PB

Hints and Hidden Depths

Proving the conjecture might involve algebra.

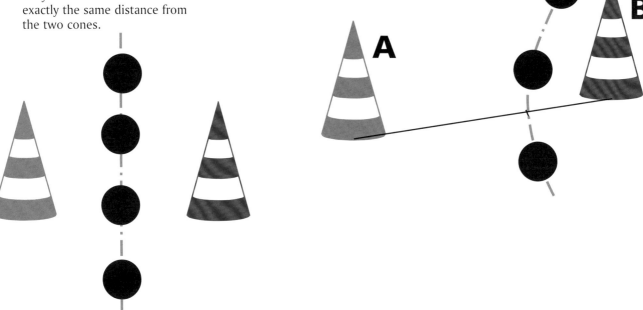

Resources needed

Lots of people

Two or even three sets of armbands or colours or team shirts/bibs

Tasks

1   People have to stand so that the angle of turn from looking at one cone to looking at the other is 90°.

2   The total distance from one cone to the other via each new person is the same (use a long rope to measure).

3   Choose, say, a long wall; a tree; a bench; a line of three desks; four desks in a square. People take up positions satisfying a given rule – e.g. must be 1 metre from the object.

4   One group of people must stand in some chosen formation e.g. in two lines which meet (we recommend initially NOT at right angles).

Another group, identifiably different, take up positions satisfying a given rule e.g. same distance from both lines.

Questions

What happens?

What shapes are created by the people's positions, assuming that one can link the points?

What can be said precisely (in mathematical language) about these newly created shapes?

Variations

Change the constraints:

in '4', have the lines intersect, rather than just meet; (here three sets of bibs help).

or in '3', introduce a rule to stand equidistant from the wall and the tree.

Hints and Hidden Depths

Take ideas back into the classroom using squared paper, plain paper – follow up with algebra if appropriate. Explore links with circle theorems, athletics tracks, conic sections, other interesting envelopes and loci.

If it is evening or at night, then you can use torches pointed downwards to be able to trace points, linking to curves.

20 CURVE STITCHING

Resources needed

Lots of people

Lots of ideally different colours of string/rope/twine – or torches

Card (ideally, laminated) with labels numbered from 0-9, 2 sets; perhaps some also from 10-36, to stand on

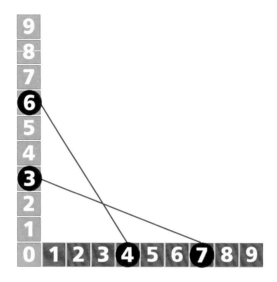

Task

Lay out cards on the ground in some chosen formation, e.g. 2 sets at right angles (as if x and y axes).

Each person involved stands on a number card.

A rule is chosen e.g. 'sum to 10'.

Pairs of people in the two different formations then hold a piece of string between them if they satisfy the chosen rule.

If this is done in the evening or at night then use torches rather than string.

Questions

What happens?

What shapes are created by the lines?

Variations

Change the arrangements:

axes not the same scale;

the two lines not at right angles – acute or obtuse angles at vertex;

lines not meeting – two parallel lines;

have one group on a line, another as if on the quadrant of a circle;

18, 24 or 36 people spread evenly round a circle with various rules for linkages – e.g. 'is double', 'is 6 more than' – use modulo arithmetic.

Hints and Hidden Depths

Use long lengths of different colours.

Take ideas back into the classroom using squared paper, plain paper – follow up with algebra if appropriate. Explore astroid, nephroid, various types of cycloids, polygons in circle, envelopes. Make links with clockface and modulo arithmetic.

Resources needed

Teams (sets) of eight

Labels numbered 1 to 8

Someone to call the changes

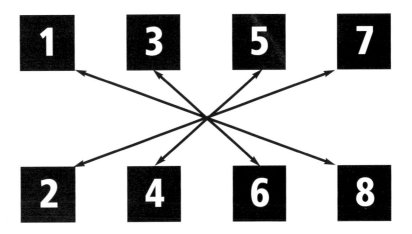

Activity

One person calls the changes.

On the call 'nines' 1 & 8 swap, 2 & 7 swap, 3 & 6 swap and 4 & 5 swap places. If possible this can be a dance move but the main thing is to ensure it is safe.

On the call 'primes' the swaps are pairs making 5 or 13; so 1– 4, 2 – 3, 5 – 8 and 6 – 7 swap.

Once the basics are understood try a sequence of moves: nines, primes, nines, primes . . .

Advanced rules

Make up some different changes and try combinations of these.

Questions

What happens?

Why?

Variations

Suppose you have nine people in an equilateral triangle and the swaps are arranged in triads; for example 3–6–9, 1–4–7, 2–5–8 might be one such change.

Hints and Hidden Depths

Link these dances with card shuffling and with group theory.

Resources needed

Teams of 5 people with cards / stickers numbered 1-5

3 lines of 5 chairs (optional)

Again you may find it helpful to appoint a number of eagle-eyed judges watching each team to ensure they stick to the rules and also to record what goes on

Task

Each group of five people starts as shown in black (sitting in the order in row A), with the aim of finishing as shown in red (sitting in the same order in row C). Person number 1 moves first.

Rules

Moves are made one person at a time.

At no time can a larger number sit in front of a smaller number in the same row.

If you join a row you must move as far back as possible to leave room in front of you for others to sit down.

Questions

How many moves are necessary?

How does this change, as the number of people changes?

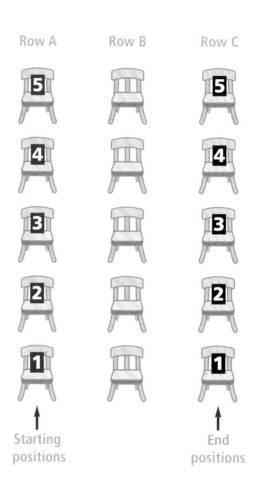

Row A   Row B   Row C

Starting positions

End positions

Hints and Hidden Depths

Recording the moves is important.

Is there a formula linking the number of moves and the number of people?

Prove that it is true.

Resources needed

6 people

12 chairs (or a grid outside)

Wall

Wall

Task

The object is to to end up with the people in reverse order in the opposite row of chairs. In other words to have person 6 on the left with person 1 on the right

Rules

A person can slide over any number of empty chairs, including any reached by going through the gap opposite chair 4 and along the bottom row to right or left.

What they cannot do is to jump over another person or cross the wall other than through the gap.

Each time a person slides it counts as one move no matter how many empty chairs are passed over.

The first move has to be 4 moving through the gap and sliding. Later in the game, 4 will have to go back and return, to complete the task.

What if . . . what if not?

Does it matter where the gap is?

Try different numbers of people.

More gaps: which are the best positions if you have two gaps?

Questions

How many moves are necessary?

How does this change, as the number of people gets larger?

Hints and Hidden Depths

You might compare this problem with traditional engine and carriage shunting problems.

Moscow Puzzles Nos 171, 172 (Boris Kordemsky)

Amusements in Mathematics (H E Dudeney) puzzle 233

The Canterbury Puzzles (H E Dudeney) puzzle 87

Resources needed

Teams of equal numbers of people

(Chairs optional but it makes it easier)

Simple equipment as necessary

Task and Rules

The session leader arranges the people into equal-sized groups.

He or she then says 'Arrange yourselves in ascending order of birth date'.

(Exclude the year . . . some of us are touchy on this subject).

Other sorting options are:

- Take the number of letters in your first name and the number of letters in your family name. Add them together.

- Take the number of letters in your first name and the number of letters in your family name. Divide the one by the other to make a number less than or equal to one.

- Head sizes (supply string).

- Hand sizes.

- Postcodes (alphabetically).

Comments

This activity is a great warm up and ideal for getting people involved.

If you want to stay sane a good idea is to get the groups to put one hand over their mouths and the other hand in the air once they are in order.

It cuts down the noise (a little) and makes it easier to see who has finished.

Hints and Hidden Depths

Compare hand-span sorting to bubble sort.

Resources needed

Teams of equal numbers of people

Start with 4 people in pairs

(2 male and 2 female or coded by coloured labels)

5 chairs

The Task

The aim is to interchange the male and female frogs in as few moves as possible.

Rules

Each frog can move in one of two ways:

- A slide to an adjoining chair.
- A hop over another frog onto an empty chair.

Questions

Can it be done?

What is the minimum number of moves?

Is there a pattern to the hops and slides?

Variations

Try different numbers of frogs, different numbers each side, different rules for hopping, different arrangements of chairs.

Hints and Hidden Depths

Find an algebraic formula for the minimum number of moves.

How would you prove your formula is true for all numbers of frogs?

Look at the pattern produced by tracing where the vacant chair is located.

Compare with TWIN TURNS and POND SWAP (Activities 8, 26).

Resources needed

6 people

7 chairs

Task

The aim is to interchange the male and female frogs getting them from one pond to another by sliding or jumping.

Rules

Moves are the same as for the classic game of FROGS (see activity 25).

Either a slide into an adjacent chair or a jump over one person on to an empty chair.

No diagonal moves are allowed.

Questions

How many moves are necessary?

How does this change, as the number of people gets larger?

What if . . . what if not?

Try different numbers of people and chairs.

Try different layouts of chairs. See below.

Hints and Hidden Depths

Is this two dimensional Frogs? It certainly adds a dimension of difficulty. A solution in 15 moves exists for the first problem.

Problems of this kind are to be found in Sam Loyd's work but they tend to involve larger numbers and are therefore of less interest as people games.

Resources needed

6 people (two teams of three)

9 chairs or a grid in a 3×3 array

Task

The game starts as in noughts and crosses. Each team places its people alternately, trying to get three in a row.

Rules

If neither team has won after these first six moves, the teams take turns to move any one of their three players to any adjacent empty square.

(Diagonal moves are not allowed.)

Variations

Try different arrangements of chairs.

Six Men's Morris played on the usual grid.

Nine Men's Morris.

Hints and Hidden Depths

Which is the best move for the first team? Why?

Which is the best move for the second team?

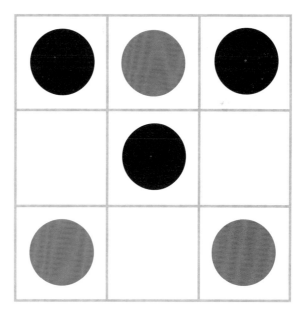

Resources needed

8 people

12 chairs as in the diagram
(3 × 4 array)

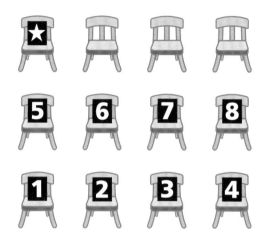

Starting point and rules

The goal with this version of solitaire is to remove people one at a time by jumping and capturing as in the normal game of solitaire. You cannot jump over a person diagonally, only 'horizontally' or 'vertically'. The aim is to finish with a person in the chair marked with a star.

Variations

Once you have successfully completed this puzzle, play reverse solitaire in which you have to put the people back on the chairs. Start with someone on the starred chair. Moves are made by someone jumping over an empty chair on to another empty chair. A new person can then sit on the chair which has been jumped over.

Try letting pupils design their own simple boards and challenging their friends to complete the puzzle.

Hints and Hidden Depths

There are lots of different boards to try including the traditional one with 33 pieces. However 33 people may not be patient enough to complete this game!

Resources needed

6 people

6 chairs, arranged in various formations

Labels 1 to 6

Task

People holding labels have to seat themselves so that no two adjacent people hold consecutive numbers.

Solutions should be recorded on (squared) paper.

Questions

Can it be done?

How many different ways can it be done for a shape/number of people?

Strategies?

Variations

Try rules such as 'at least a gap of 3 between the numbers on the labels of adjacent people'.

Try other arrangements of people and shapes, e.g. 8 people arranged in 'a square with a hole in the middle'; 9 people in a square formation; for each, gaps ≥ 2 or ≥ 3.

Hints and Hidden Depths

See also 'SEPARATES' (Activity 30).

Resources needed

Teams of equal numbers of people. Four in a team is a good starting point.

You may find it helpful to appoint a number of eagle-eyed managers watching each team to ensure they stick to the rules.

Task

Each person only uses one arm.

The object is to get from the starting position in which all arms are down to one in which each person has their arm up.

Rules

Left and right refer to how it is if you are part of the group . . . the pictures show the group facing you.

The person on the extreme left of the group (D) can move their arm up or down at any stage.

The others can ONLY move their arm up or down when the immediate neighbour on their left has their arm down AND all the other people further to the left have their arm up.

Not all the steps are illustrated.

RIGHT   LEFT

START

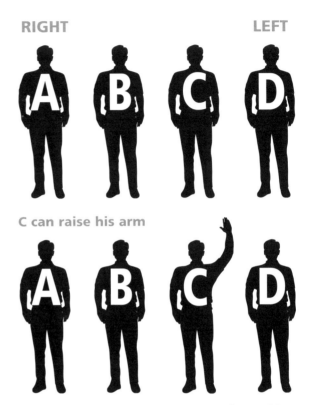

C can raise his arm

In order for A to move, B must have his arm down whilst C and D have their arm up

How can B get to raise his arm?

If C puts his arm down then B can raise his

Now if D puts his arm down, C can raise his

D can then raise his arm, achieving the objective

FINISH

Variations

Try smaller groups of people.

Try larger groups.

Try different rules. For example: The two people on the extreme left can move their arm up or down at any stage.

The others can ONLY move their arm up or down when the two immediate neighbours on their left have their arm down AND all the other people further to the left have their arm up.

Questions

One move is a person raising or lowering an arm. How many moves are necessary?

How does this change as the number of people gets larger?

Hints and Hidden Depths

For this puzzle the number of moves forms an interesting recurrence relationship depending on the number of people.

For four people it is possible to get all arms up in 10 moves.

Resources needed

5-10 people

Cards 1 to 10 (or labels)

Task

Arrange people in a circle holding cards so that no two adjacent people hold consecutive numbers.

Rules

Recommendation to ask people to go and take their place in turn, i.e. use a form of trial and improvement.

Questions

Can it be done?

How many different ways are possible for a given number of people?

Strategies?

Variations

Try fewer/more people.

Try rules such as 'at least a gap of 2 (i.e. 3 – 6) between the numbers on the cards of adjacent people'.

Try other arrangements of people, e.g. in a cross pattern, or in a line.

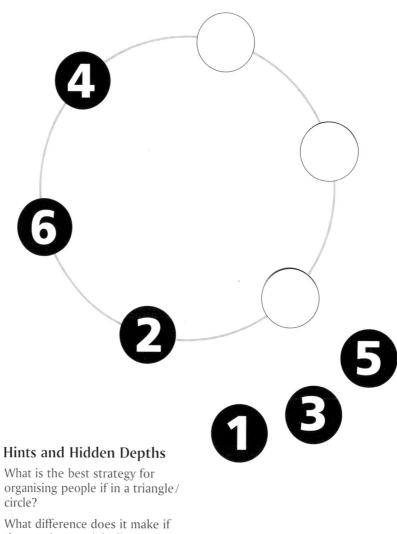

Hints and Hidden Depths

What is the best strategy for organising people if in a triangle / circle?

What difference does it make if they are in a straight line, or in the form of a cross (i.e. with one person in both lines)?

See also 'NEIGHBOURS' (Activity 29).

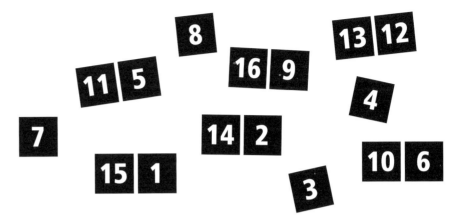

Resources needed

An even number of people. [Be aware: some numbers are not 'good'!] (26 or more is when it can be great!)

Labels numbered from 1 up to the largest number are given to all involved.

Task

Each person is labelled, and stands. Check whether 'square number' and 'pair' are understood by everyone.

The task is for everyone to pair up so that the sum of the two numbers they 'are' makes a square number.

People pair up if they can, and sit if paired. If some have not been paired off, then use trial and improvement – i.e. they nominate with whom they want to pair, and take the place of that one's current partner. The displaced person now comes out.

The important issue is for everyone to have paired up before it is a successful activity, and that trial and improvement means you don't just restart. Recording is important too.

Questions

Which (even) numbers can be square paired?

Which cannot? (Do 6 as an example)

Which can be square paired so that 1 matches the largest, 2 matches one less etc. (e.g. 8 via 1-8, 2-7, 3-6, 4-5)?
Is there a pattern to these numbers?

Which can be square paired more than one way?

Different rules

Try pairs with different rules e.g. making a triangle number, a cube, an even number or one divisible by three.

Try triples of people.

Hints and Hidden Depths

Try 18, 8, 16, 14, 24 and 26 as a people activity, if possible, before moving to pencil and paper trials for other numbers. Record the square pairs solutions.

It is worth discussing between first attempt to pair off, and before beginning trial and improvement, if there are some numbers that can only be matched with one other (e.g. when square pairing 14, 9 can only be paired with 7).

Explore numbers one less than an odd square. Explore multiples of 8. Are these two connected? It may be worth algebraic exploration of this if the ability of the class warrants.

There are just 7 even numbers which cannot be square paired. It is worth exploring proofs for the smaller ones to show that they are impossible.

All even numbers greater than 24 can be square paired.

All even numbers from 26 inclusive can be square paired in more than one way; 26 has 6 solutions, it can be a nice task to try to find them all.

See Chapter 3.

33 TRIPLES

Resources needed

6 people

Labels numbered from 1 to 6

Task

People with cards arrange themselves so that the sum along each side of the triangle is the same.

Questions

In how many different ways can it be done?

Strategies?

How many changes?

Which totals are possible?

Variations

Try with 9 people, 4 on each side of the triangle.

Try other numbers of people (so the sides don't have the same number of people).

Try other shapes – e.g. 8 people in a square formation.

Hints and Hidden Depths

Explore maximum and minimum totals possible, and implications for which numbers can and can't be in corners.

Explore 'complementary' situations.

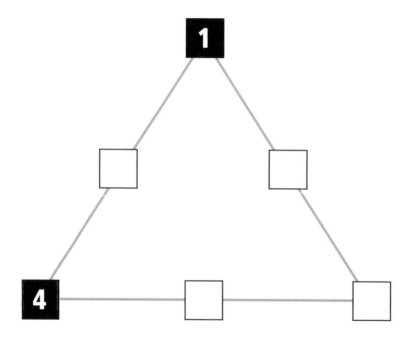

Resources needed

6 people (per team)

Labels numbered 1 to 6

It can help to have a team manager

Task

Each person (in a team of 6) is labelled with a number 1 to 6.

The 6 people form themselves into pairs, as they wish.

Suppose the pairs are (1,3), (2,4) and (5,6).

The product of each pair is calculated and then, for each team, the sum of the products. This is the team score.

In the example the team score would be $1 \times 3 + 2 \times 4 + 5 \times 6$ or 41.

Questions

What is the maximum total?

What is the minimum total?

What totals are possible?

Different rules

Try with threes getting together, then finding sum of product.

Try finding the product of the three sums of pairs.

Try other starting numbers of people.

Try other number labels on people.

Hints and Hidden Depths

It will be important to record and discuss the results, and the reasons for people's choices of strategy, preferably with some analysis, so it's more than a game.

35 NUMBER SANDWICHES

Resources needed

An even number of people 2-16

A chair per person

2 sets of labels each numbered from 1 up to half the number taking part

Task

A 'number sandwich' is successfully formed if everyone involved is paired in such a way that the number of people between a person and their number pair is that number; e.g. if a '3 sandwich' is to be formed, 6 people (3 pairs labelled 1,2,3) are to be seated so that between the two 3s there are 3 people; between the two 2s there are 2 people, and between the two 1s there is one person.

Questions

What number sandwiches are possible?

Which number sandwiches are impossible? (Proof?)

Which number sandwiches can be formed in more than one different way? (Consider, but perhaps ignore, reverses.)

What starting strategies are best to start trying to form a number sandwich?

Different rules

Consider people not in a line but in a circle.

Hints and Hidden Depths

Try with 3, 2, 1, 4, 5, 6, 7 pairs of people (some possible, some not; 7 possible in quite a few ways, 8 similarly. The 'NRICH' website mentions this game: www.nrich.maths.org.uk

Resources needed

7 or more people to form a number train

Cards 1 to 6 (even 1-9, at least one of each), at least three labelled 0, and one with a decimal point

It would help to have labelled cards/posters e.g TTh, Th, H, T, U, dp, t, h, th, or the actual place value words they represent, displayed behind those holding numbers

Start with, for example:

Task

A number is chosen by the 'caller', and people arrange themselves to make that number.

The 'caller' manages the individuals' rearrangement into a correct number having chosen the arithmetic processes.

e.g. from a start of 16.0020, try in sequence
$\times 100$
$\div 1000$
$\times 10000$
-10001
$+20$
-21
$\div 5$
$\times 10$
$\div 2$
$+10.2$

There needs to be some planning of the processes by the caller in order for the cardholders to be able to calculate the answer, its representation, and hence the moves needed.

Questions

What is a good start number, that allows a good few simple processes to be used consecutively, while retaining largely the same numbers as answers?

What, then, are the processes?

Different rules

Try other numbers as starting positions.

Try to find other processes leading to simple changes from one number (as a group in a line) to the next.

Hints and Hidden Depths

It is essential to get the message across that the decimal point does not move.

It helps to get the message across that when numbers get a power of 10 times bigger, the number train moves 'forward'; if divided by a power of 10, getting smaller, it moves backwards.

Other than that, this gives a chance for some mental mathematics.

Resources needed

Teams of five people, each team has a set of ten large cards marked 0 to 9

A caller with a set of ten bingo balls marked 0 to 9 in a bag

Each team has a row of five chairs in front of them

Task

The aim of the game is for the team to get the highest possible number from the arrangement of the five digits which are called.

A ball is picked out of the bag by the 'caller'.

One of each team then selects that number card and sits down on one of the chairs, following a short discussion with the rest of the team. The caller quickly checks that every team has a person sat down with a number clearly showing. Once seated that person remains there till the end of the whole round.

The caller repeats the process four more times so that all members of the teams are sat down with five cards in order. The example above would be a poor choice if the numbers were called in the order: 5, 7, 6, 2, 0.

Since the aim of the game was to get the highest possible number, they should have chosen to sit down as 76520.

Variations

A   Try getting:

1   the largest even number

2   the largest odd number

3   the smallest number

4   the smallest even number

5   the smallest odd number

B

Try the game with the caller using a ten-sided die (or replacing the balls each time). You will need more cards of course because a number can come up several times, not just once.

C

Try getting the largest product of a two digit and three digit number as below.

This time 76×520 wouldn't be the largest value.

Resources needed

Lots of people

100 carpet tiles (ask at your local carpet shop or superstore for stuff which would otherwise be thrown out) or squares large enough to be stood on by a person

Number these tiles 1–100, and (initially) lay them out to form a 100-square

It would help to have the ATM publication 10^2

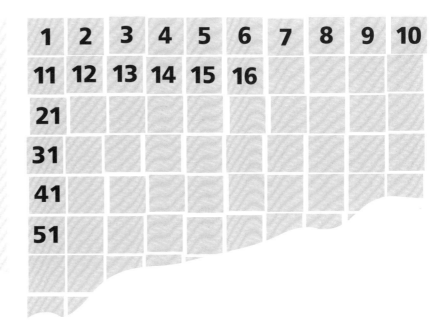

Task

Each person initially stands on a square of their choice, aware of which number they have chosen to stand on, and how the numbers are laid out around them.

The 'caller' gives various instructions and people move to the appropriate square. Discuss with participants the movements involved, and how one can work out mentally (without looking down) how to move.

Use instructions like add 1, add 5, add 20, take away 10, add 19, take 11, add 28, take 13 etc.

Questions

What are the simplest processes?

Are there different ways to get the required moves? Are they equally 'good'?

Different rules

People are asked to stand on various 'times table' positions – e.g. to form even numbers, 5 times table, multiples of 7, 9, 11, square numbers; primes notice patterns (or lack of them).

Use different layouts e.g. 'snakes and ladders' format for the 100 squares.

Hints and Hidden Depths

Ensure that later all work is recorded on the pupils' own 100 squares.

Try doing Sieve of Eratosthenes (to find prime numbers) 'live'.

Use a 6-column version to show all primes >3 are of form $6n\pm1$.

Resources needed

Lots of people

100 carpet tiles (ask at your local carpet shop or superstore for stuff which would otherwise be thrown out) or squares large enough to be stood on by a person

Number these tiles 1–100, and (initially) lay them out to form a 100-square

It would help to have the ATM publication 10^2

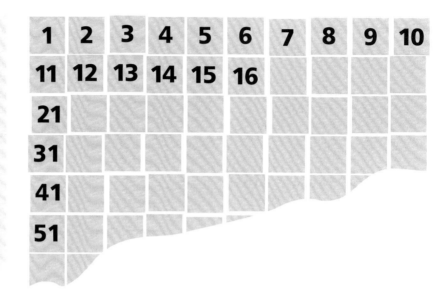

39A SPIDER GAME

Using the carpet tile layout illustrated, each person stands on a square of their choice.

The 'caller' then gives the following instructions:

> If your number is even, divide by two and then move to that square;

> If your number is odd, times by 3 and then add 1.

> If you go over 100 you are out. If you land on square 1 the spider gets you and you are out.

What happens? Who lasts the longest?

39B DIGITAL PRODUCT

Using the carpet tile layout illustrated, each person stands on a square of their choice.

If your square is 10a + b then you multiply a by b and move to the square with that number on it.

So for example if you are on square numbered 73 you will move to 21.

Square with a single digit (8 for example) will be treated as $0 \times$ the digit and end up as a product of 0.

You are out when your product equals 0.

Where is the best place to stand if you want to last longest?

Hints and Hidden Depths

It may be an idea to tackle this by creating a chain of numbers leading to the end number. Alternatively this might be a spreadsheet exercise.

Resources needed

Lots of people, in teams of about 7-10

Open space preferably with squared, or easily measurable, grid

Sets of cards with single LOGO instructions e.g. FD 2, BK 2, RT 90, LT 90, FD 4, BK 4, RT 180

FD 2

RT 90°

FD 3

LT 90°

BK 4

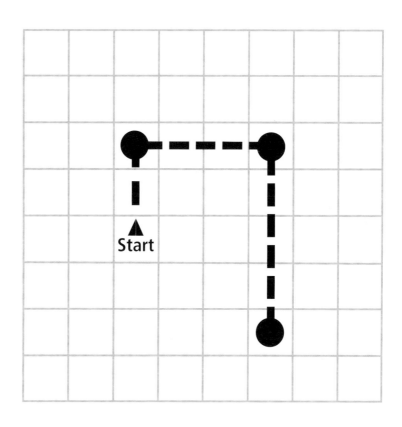

Task

Cards are given out, 1 per person in a team.

Teams initially investigate where they get to by following instructions in turn, each person starting where the last one finished.

(Later on these moves should be recorded on squared paper).

You need to decide on a consistent '1 unit'.

Questions

What end locations are possible?

Are there many ways to get to the same result?

Is a closed loop, i.e. ending back where you started, possible?

How can you get furthest away from where you started?

Variations

More cards, more complicated cards.

(For example, cards with a combination of 1 move and 1 turn.)

41 MOLECULES

Resources needed

A large number of people, split into teams, ideally but not necessarily all the same size. 10, 6 are good initial starting numbers

Someone to 'manage' and record the results for each team

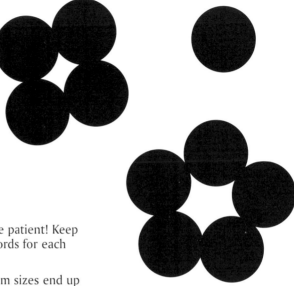

Task

Teams are formed of, say, 10 people per team.

The task is for the team to split into molecules, and then to form new ones.

The initial split is free choice – as shown in the diagram, for example, into 4, 5 and 1.

From then on, in each new round, one person from each current molecule splits off to form a new molecule.

The number of people in each molecule at the end of each round is recorded. This is important!

Keep going until you reach either 'steady state' or repeat.

Questions

What happens? (Be patient! Keep looking at the records for each round).

Which starting team sizes end up as 'steady state' – i.e. the new molecules formed in the next round are the same as this round. What, then, are the sizes of the steady state molecules?

Which team sizes do not give 'steady state' but repeat to form molecule groups of sizes met in earlier rounds (loops)?

Hints and Hidden Depths

It is often useful to have one member of the team recording what happens.

Explore triangle-number-sized teams first (1, 3, 6, 10, 15, etc), then other numbers.

Resources needed

A line of numbers from, say, $^-10$ to $^+10$; it works well if the numbers are on paper cut-outs of clothing, strung out as a washing line, across the front of the classroom. It helps if there is an arrow pointing 'forward' in the direction that the numbers increase

Task

The teacher asks a pupil to stand at a number. All such initial positions should face 'forwards'.

Moving '$^+2$' is explored from a range of starting points which should include positive and negative numbers, and zero. Moving 0 is recognised as not moving.

Explore moving '$^-2$' in two ways, initially best from position '$^+3$', or '$^+5$'. First, as moving backwards two places. Then, as seeing the '$^-$' as telling you to turn round, then go two places. Try also, for example, $3-(^-3)$, or $^-3+3$.

Once the equivalence of the above two processes is understood, you can explore, for example, $^+3 - (^-2)$ via using 'turn round', also $^-2-(^-3)$, etc.

Ask pupils to set various such tasks. The 'caller' gives instructions and people move to the square appropriate. Discuss with participants the movements involved, and how to work out instructions $3+(^-3)$, etc.

Questions

What are the simplest processes?

Are there different ways to get the required moves? Are they equally 'good'?

Variations

It can be worth exploring the alternative approach using nomograms: 3 parallel axes, with the middle one double scale. When two numbers on the outside two scales are linked by a line, the middle axis gives the answer to their addition.

Thanks to Emma Carter at St Paul's RC School, Sunbury for the idea.

Hints and Hidden Depths

Ensure all later work is recorded, perhaps getting pupils to draw their own clothes line/number line.

43 ORCHESTRA

Resources needed

Lots of people

It can help to have labels 1 to N, i.e. one for each person in the activity

Tasks

People are given numbers from 1 up to N.

The 'caller' calls out numbers in turn. The first time it may be best to do this from 1 in sequence.

People have to stand up if their number is a factor of the called number; i.e. if the called number is a multiple of theirs.

The participants should keep track of those standing up, both which actual numbers and how many stand up, and when i.e. in response to which called numbers.

Thanks to Emma Carter at St Paul's RC School, Sunbury for the idea

Questions

What happens?

Ask questions of participants, such as:

Who stands up every time?

Who stands up and stays seated alternately?

When do only two people stand up?

When will there be an odd number of people standing up?

Variations

Try having the participants arranged in sequence. Does it clarify some of the questions?

Try having each person make a prearranged noise (if in appropriately soundproofed environment).

Invent other rules for standing up or making a noise.

Hints and Hidden Depths

Take ideas back into the classroom using '100 squares' and/or squared paper.

It could help to have read the ATM publication 10^2.

Compare with 'CARPET TILES – 100 SQUARES' (Activity 38).

3 Notes on some of the activities

Bob's Story of Square Pairs
(ACTIVITY 32)

Square Pairs as an activity initially evolved as a result of my contribution to a Mathematics Masterclass. This involved investigating square numbers, and Pythagoras' Theorem – exploring which square numbers could be made as a sum of two square numbers.

As part of the first session to the PGCE Secondary mathematics course for which I was course leader, I like to have paired introductions, and wish to organise the group, usually around 30 people, into pairs of people who generally do not know each other. It is conducive to setting up a whole group ethos to mix people up so that they can make new friends to add to those they may have known before or met at interview. Some form of sorting process, preferably mathematical, is needed.

It is easy to number people 1 to N and match them so they come to the same total; e.g. if there were 26 then they all paired with their '27-complement', i.e. the number with which they combined to

make 27. When there were 24 in the group, this strategy gave '25-complements', each pair added to make 25, interestingly a square number. When the group of 24 were split into three groups each numbered 1-8, again they could each sum not just to the same number (9) but one which was again a square. It followed after some discussion that some numbers one less than a square, like 8, 24, 48, 120 – actually all numbers one less than an odd square – would work very nicely in this way, all pairs giving the same square total.

Trying with 16 people led to the discovery that we could match 16 with 9, 15 with 10, and so on making 25s, and then be left with the numbers 1 to 8 which we knew (from before) would pair to make 9. So, we discovered that some even numbers could be square paired if we allowed the totals to be different squares.

We tried to see if '14' (using people numbered 1 to 14) would 'square pair' by matching along the lines of going for 'largest first' (14, 11), (13, 12) (10, 6) (9, 7) (8, 1) (5, 4) – oops! We are left with 3 and 2!

For some this 'stuck' situation suggested trying again from the beginning, which the majority felt not to be a good mathematical strategy. Some others reasoned: why not try 'trial and improvement' without destroying all we have? It was so nice to have an example for a practical use of trial and improvement strategy that was not just for the solution of equations! (See the Mathematics National Curriculum documents).

One or two voices pointed out that if it was to work, i.e. if we were to be able to square pair all the 14 people, then 10 must be matched with 6; 9 with 7; and 8 with 1. No other ways of making a square total were possible for 10, 9, or 8, here. So – first we got 3 to pair up with 13, releasing 12; similarly 14 got paired with 2 releasing 11. The solution now stared us in the face: if we split the (5,4) pairing, we could match 11 with 5, and 12 with 4 – and all of 1-14 were 'square paired'.

'18' worked in a similar way, though needed a bit more trial and patience. If we did it as a people game, or later did it using pencil and paper, it was especially helpful to notice almost before starting that 18 needed to match with 7, 17 with 8, and 16 with 9. So far so good, but then 15 gave us a choice of 10 or 1, and choices needed to be made. The strategy of pairing the largest numbers first seemed to be most effective, though some did try either more randomly or by starting with 1. It was agreed virtually unanimously that initially it could be wise to try to make the largest squares as sums of the pairs.

When this activity is done as a people game, (see the guidance elsewhere in the book) it seems to work best that once numbered people stand to start with; a 'free for all' pairing attempt is made and people sit in pairs once they have found a suitable partner. It is then important to see that the solution must involve everybody being paired, to overcome the anxiety both of those initially left standing, unpaired, and those later being separated from what they had thought was a perfectly suitable partner. This latter process seems to work best if we start with the largest number standing, who then swaps places with someone by finding a pair with whom to sit. The displaced person needs to stand up, and as pairs arise among those standing, we find trial and improvement normally leads eventually to everyone being seated, square paired.

'26' was interesting since in the group's first attempt at a solution as a people game, someone made an error in copying down the result, and after showing some persistence came up with a different solution to the original one we had found. So far we had only found unique solutions. To our amazement, a third person came up with yet another solution, and eventually we discovered that '26' can be square paired in 6 different ways. It is actually the first number that is not uniquely 'soluble'.

It was surmised that many, perhaps most, even numbers should be able to be square paired, i.e. that it was often possible to pair everyone in a whole group of people who had been numbered 1 to N by having them pair up so their total was a square number. On the other hand, we discovered trying 12 people numbered 1-12 would not lead to a complete set of square pairs. Clearly, though, some other even numbers cannot be square paired either: e.g. '6' (6 must be paired with 3, 5 with 4, and we are stuck with 'unpairable' 2 and 1 – and so '2' can't be square paired either!). Actually we discovered there were just 7 even numbers which could not be square paired.

The above describes much of the first, and of course many subsequent, introductory sessions of this activity. Some people to whom this was introduced went away and did some powerful mathematics as a result. Johnston Anderson at Nottingham University, wrote his work in a copy of the *Mathematical Gazette*, (Vol 83, No.496, 1999) published by the Mathematical Association. There is a proof that all even numbers greater than 24 can be square paired, indeed all in more than one way. Among other nice results are generalisations to square pairing 'one less than odd squares' – all of which are multiples of 8 (as can quite easily be proved by secondary school level algebra). Also multiples of 8 are those numbers like '16', the solution of which contains a subset of a lower number square pairing – another is '32' – a solution to which pairs 32-17, always to make 49; and leaves 1-16 we already know we can square pair.

Sam Costello wrote an article in ATM's *Mathematics Teaching* magazine (No.170, March 2000) about a visit he made to the Falklands teaching mathematics. He used variations to sort groups of pupils via people games, matching to triangular numbers, prime numbers, and other rules. In many a mathematics conference, ATM, SMILE, BCME, and in school halls and classrooms on Maths days, large groups of people have actively, kinæsthetically, learnt about the fun, and the mathematics, of square pairing. Let's hope you and people with whom you try this activity will too.

Shuffles – some anecdotes and advice from Bob

There is much fun that can be had by using variations of Shuffles. The name itself conjures up the use of playing cards, which is where some of the shuffle ideas in this book originated. There is a recognisable need in 'the real world' for lists to be put into order, whether alphabetical, numerical, size or by some other rule, and ways in which a list can be ordered, or re-ordered, by using some rule or process for the rearrangement. This seems to provide a good practical reason for exploring what, here, are just called shuffles.

An experience of these shuffles came for me when given the task of working with a small group of ten promising mathematicians aged 10 and 11, Year 5 & 6, at a junior school. As a mathematics curriculum support teacher in the London Borough of Hillingdon, a part of my role was to provide enrichment activities for able pupils in the borough's schools. The school had asked if I could try to use activities linking in with their current topic theme, of *The Land*. Exploring what mathematics related to this theme was not obvious!

I recalled some of a university statistics course which I had found interesting, where crop rotation patterns across a given number of fields had been investigated by the statistician R A Fisher at the Government's Agricultural Experimental Research Station at Rothamsted. It is necessary for a farmer to change the crop he grows on a field, as the useful chemicals 'leach' out of the soil in any one year, helping the crop grow, and so will not be there in the same quantity the following year, leading to a poorer crop. Hence the benefit of rotating crops between a group of fields. If the simplest rotation is used, say in a set of four fields, (say a, b, c, d) so that crop 1 is always followed by crop 2, 2 by 3, 3 by 4, 4 by 1, this can be represented diagrammatically as below:

Fields	a	b	c	d
Year 0	1	2	3	4
Year 1	2	3	4	1
Year 2	3	4	1	2
Year 3	4	1	2	3

It should now be clear that the next row would bring us back to the original arrangement. This above is an example of a 'Latin square' – a square table where each item appears once and only once in every row and column – here of order 4, as there are 4 items. These Latin squares appear often (but not always!) if a similar approach to the recording of shuffles is used. This is also an example of a 'cyclic group' in group theory, a part of the Modern Algebra course normally covered in university mathematics degrees, and worthy of further investigation.

It is worth noting that this table is symmetrical about its leading diagonal (top left to bottom right) indicating that there is likely to be an underlying commutative process. Unlike those tables for addition and multiplication with which we are most familiar, it should not be assumed that tables generated in this way to record our shuffles will always be symmetrical – or even cyclic.

It was discovered that the chemicals leached from one crop would always affect the quality of the next crop, and so the above arrangement was not ideal, since having the successor crop the same every time would always diminish its potential. What was needed was to find an arrangement where, ideally, crop 1 sown in a field would be followed by different crops over the years. Unfortunately this proves difficult for 'fields' of order less than 6.

So learning from the above, if we try a shuffle, it may be best to record results in a similar way. If we try a CUT SHUFFLE, (Activity 10) – e.g. having 6 people with a cut of 4, (i.e. the first 4 items, in the list of 6, move to the back) – then one can notice that it takes 3 rounds to return to the original formation. One can ignore either the first or the last row in this counting of rounds.

Initial	1	2	3	4	5	6
after round 1	5	6	1	2	3	4
after round 2	3	4	5	6	1	2
after round 3	1	2	3	4	5	6

A cut shuffle, with 6 initial items, of 5 (or 1) leads us to a table of order 6, as below:

Initial	1	2	3	4	5	6
after round 1	6	1	2	3	4	5
after round 2	5	6	1	2	3	4
after round 3	4	5	6	1	2	3
after round 4	3	4	5	6	1	2
after round 5	2	3	4	5	6	1
after round 6	1	2	3	4	5	6

It is worth noting that this table is not symmetrical about its leading diagonal (top left to bottom right); for tables of order 6 or greater such symmetry does not always occur.

Another shuffle which proved interesting and instructive to explore I first met as a puzzle at an ATM Easter course session run by Ian Harris and Lyndon Baker. We were shown a set of 6 cards, numbered 1 to 6, clearly not quite in numerical order. The first card, number 1, was taken from the front and placed on the table. The next card was put at the back of the remaining cards. The next one at the front was a 2, and it was placed on the table, then the following one was placed at the back of the pack. This process, one card laid on the table, the next placed at the back, continued until we had all the cards on the table.

They were found to be in numerical order, 1-6, and our puzzle was to find in what order we had started with the cards to get this numerically ordered sequence. (If we were able to do that, we were told we should discover in what order to place 1-8, or 1-10, in order to achieve a correct numerical sequence using this 'one down, one to the back' process.)

The BIG step to discovering the solution was that, if we started with 1-6 in correct order, then by repeatedly shuffling the pack according the same process, we should return to the original numerical sequence. The penultimate ordering of the six cards would give the one which, when the dealing process was applied, would lead to the cards being in correct numerical order.

Applying the process to 1-6 in correct order, we can track what happens either via

1 down, 2 to the back, 3 down, 4 to the back, 5 down, 6 to the back (there are then just 3 cards remaining, 2, 4, 6 in order) so 2 down, 4 to the back, 6 down, and then only 4 remains, so 4 down.

We can tabulate the sequence formed as

Initial	1	2	3	4	5	6
after round 1	1	3	5	2	6	4

If the process is repeated we get

Initial	1	2	3	4	5	6
after round 1	1	3	5	2	6	4
after round 2	1	5	6	3	4	2

Now we can keep doing this until we complete the table, i.e. until we end up with a row identical to the first or (I recommend) notice a short cut. Notice that below 1 is a 1 (each time). Notice also that in the first two rows, below 2 is a 3, below 3 is 5, below 5 is 6, below 6 is 4 and below 4 is 2. If we start with 2 then in successive places in the column beginning 2 should be, in sequence, 3, 5, 6, 4, then 2. This suggests how we can fill in the table after just one round. It should guide us as to how many rounds, and lines, should be necessary (and whether we get a Latin square).

Initial	1	2	3	4	5	6
after round 1	1	3	5	2	6	4
after round 2	1	5	6	3	4	2
after round 3	1	6	4	5	2	3
after round 4	1	4	2	6	3	5
after round 5	1	2	3	4	5	6

So firstly we now know this is a shuffle which returns to its original order after 5 rounds; but also we know that as a solution to the original puzzle, we need the cards to be in the order (as in the penultimate round of the shuffle) 1, 4, 2, 6, 3, 5. We can also see that we have produced a Latin square of order 5 with the numbers 2-6.

One might usefully reflect that since the 1 is always the first down, there are only 5 cards to shuffle and so it makes sense that it should take (no more than) 5 rounds to get back to the starting sequence.

A final word of warning, however: it can be presumptuous to assume that this sort of logic will always be appropriate. Sometimes in mathematics it is dangerous to make predictions based on a limited number of examples.

As an example: if one tries doing BACK-FRONT SHUFFLES (Activity 11) with say 5 or 6 people, a 'rule' appears to be quickly arising to be able to predict after how many rounds the sequence returns to its original order. With 5 it takes 5 rounds, with 6 it takes 6 rounds. There will be those who now assume that it takes as many rounds as the number of people. With 8 people however, it does something unexpected, as illustrated below in the table.

Back Front Shuffle using 8 people

1	2	3	4	5	6	7	8
8	1	7	2	6	3	5	4
4	8	5	1	3	7	6	2
2	4	6	8	7	5	3	1
1	2	3	4	5	6	7	8

I leave to the reader to explore for which other starting numbers this unexpected faster completion, return to the original sequence, occurs, and why. Some interesting patterns are noticeable in the tables, and are worth investigating.

The prediction of a general formula for number of rounds for a given number of people is quite a challenge for this shuffle, as it is for some of the others in this book.

Alan's Tale of Infinite Series ... involving the Royal Institution in Basingstoke, Archimedes in New York, & the Royal Society (ACTIVITY 18)

I taught students about the sum to infinity of certain geometric series for many years in what I would call a traditional way. This involved the neat trick of multiplying a GP by its common ratio and then subtracting.

If a is the first term of the series and r is the common ratio and S the sum to infinity. Then

$$S = a + ar + ar^2 + ar^3 + ar^4 + ...$$

$$rS = ar + ar^2 + ar^3 + ar^4 + ar^5 + ...$$

$$(1-r) S = a$$

$$S = a / (1-r)$$

I had wanted to develop a more practical way of introducing this topic and soon came across the folding paper activity which involved a large A1 sheet of paper, which could be folded in half and opened out. Then one half could be folded again and opened out leaving a quarter to be folded and so on producing folds which could be emphasised using a felt tip to show that the sum of the series

$1/2 + 1/4 + 1/8 + 1/16 + ...$ got closer and closer to 1

When invited by Jenny Jones to run a Royal Institution Mathematics Masterclass for Y9 pupils in Basingstoke, I decided to turn this into a people maths activity and came up with activity 18. Instead of folding the paper, two people stood at opposite sides of the large hall we were working in and one person moved towards the other. Naturally the distance decreasing between them caused some amusement and a stop was called. I then set the task of inventing a way of finding out and then demonstrating practically what the sum to infinity would be of the series

$1/3 + 1/9 + 1/27 + 1/81 + ...$

One of the groups came up with the suggestion of two people moving towards each other taking equal jumps each time. At each step they move one third of the remaining distance towards each other. Soon they meet together and can imagine the process continuing so that they have each taken half the total distance, showing that the series sums to 1/2. The 'fractal' feel to this solution is very attractive. However much you zoom in the moves look the same.

I then developed ways of adapting this to work for other geometric series.

The link with Archimedes came about when I went to the 50th Annual Conference of AMTNYS (the Association of Mathematics Teachers of New York State) in October 2000 to run a workshop on People Maths. Travelling at the last minute left me arriving without a break, late on the first day of the conference, but I quickly found a session to attend on the Lost Book of Archimedes – the Palimpsest[1]. The speaker, Gary Towsley of SUNY Geneseo, described how the book had been rediscovered and by way of illustration of its contents put up the following diagram, which Archimedes had used as part of a lemma with the intention of showing that

$$1/4 + 1/16 + 1/64 + 1/256 + \ldots$$
has a sum to infinity of $1/3$.

The grey upside down L shape has to be seen as having an area of

unity. Then the successive dark and light red shapes have areas of 1/4, 1/16 and so on. Adding their areas together they make a square which is one third of the largest grey L shape.

This diagram and the proof it contains had a dramatic effect; I wanted to have a word with Archimedes. Over two thousand two hundred years were as nothing as the power of Archimedes' demonstration immediately struck home. No wonder his famous last words are reported to be "Don't disturb my circles". The power of the visual in mathematics is too often understated.

Postscript to this tale

I have been involved in friendly discussion about the nature of proof with others. Some dismiss activities such as the one here on Infinite Series and diagrammatical 'proofs' such as that by Archimedes. My view was that if it was good enough for Archimedes, it would probably do for my students. However at a Royal Society Discussion Meeting in October 2004 on the Nature of Mathematical Proof, I came across the work of Mateja Jamnik[2] which helps to bridge the gap between these non-formal methods and formal proof.

Perhaps inadvertently the Royal Society may be seen to be responsible for a similar bridging across the divide between what works in schools and what is acceptable to University mathematics departments.

Alan & the String Game: seeing things differently
(ACTIVITY 17)

This activity seems fairly complicated at first. If the diagram below can be represented by the number chain 1 3 6 5 2 4, then pegs would be attached to each section of the string as follows depending on the difference between the numbers at each end. This would give 2 pegs for the section joining people numbered 1 and 3, with 3, 1, 3, 2 and 3 pegs on the other sections, giving a total of 14 pegs. There are a large number of possible ways of connecting up the people to give such a total.

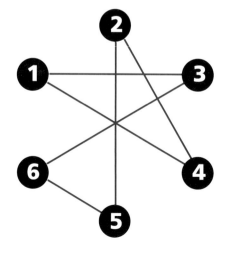

1 See www.thewalters.org/archimedes for more about the Palimpsest

2 Jamnik M. (2001) *Mathematical Reasoning with Diagrams: From Intuition to Automation*, Stanford CA, CSLI Press

How can we work out what is the smallest total and how can we be sure that it is the smallest?

One way might be to be very systematic and record all possible permutations of the six numbers.

However if we change the diagram by putting the six people in order in a straight line an equal distance apart, then everything becomes clearer.

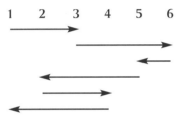

The number pegs are just the same numerically as the distance between the people in standard units, so the shortest distance connecting people up is to go straight from 1 to 6 and return. This is also represented by the permutation 1 2 3 4 5 6 which gives a total of 10 made up of 5×1 unit and a 5 unit length.

At first it might seem that this is the only way of getting the shortest distance or smallest number of pegs. However 1 3 5 6 4 2 also gives a total of 10. Why does this happen? Quite simply the journey is the same, but the stops are visited in a different order.

So, seeing a problem differently can be the difference between seeing it and not seeing it at all. We need to encourage holistic thinking as well as systematic step-by-step investigation. Thinking visually as well as algebraically can help us to make the problem soluble for many learners. As teachers in today's classrooms we need to cater more completely for the variety of pupils' learning styles, be they aural, visual or kinæsthetic, holistic or step-by-step, in order to ensure maximum benefit to them as learners. Perhaps also in fulfilling their variety of learning needs, we add to the potential for innovation in our own teaching and learning.

4 Additional places to look for ideas

The two main mathematics teachers' professional subject associations in the UK, namely The Association of Teachers of Mathematics (ATM), and The Mathematical Association (MA), both have interesting periodicals and websites. Explore these to provide further ideas both in how some of the activities in this book have been adapted or put into use, and other activities you can adapt into a People Maths activity.

Their websites are www.atm.org.uk and www.m-a.org.uk; their publications currently include ATM's *Mathematics Teaching* and *Micromath*, and the MA's *Mathematics in School* and *Plus*.

The Millennium Mathematics Project, based at the University of Cambridge, has a number of incorporated websites worth exploring for activities probably much more fun to do as people games than as solitary, or seated whole class, activity. Explore www.mmp.maths.org, www.nrich.maths.org, www.plus.maths.org, and www.motivate.maths.org.

Explore also The University of Exeter-based Centre for Innovation in Mathematics Teaching, via www.ex.ac.uk/cimt/

Other countries also have associations and websites worth exploring, including:

In Australia, Maths300 project and linked sites www.blackdouglas.co.au/project.htm

In Northern Ireland, curriculum development ideas via www.nine.org.uk/index.asp

In the USA, the National Council of Teachers of Mathematics, www.nctm.org

Books to explore

Creative Puzzles of the World, Pieter van Delft and Jack Botermans, Cassell, 1978

Mind Benders Games of Chance, Ivan Moscovich, Penguin, 1986

The Moscow Puzzles, Boris A Kordemsky, Pelican, 1975

Amusements in Mathematics, H E Dudeney, Dover, 1970

The Canterbury Puzzles, H E Dudeney, Dover, 1958

Puzzle-Math, George Gamow & Marvin Stern, Macmillan, 1960

Mathematical Recreations & Essays, W W Rouse Ball, Macmillan, 1959

The Penguin Book of Curious and Interesting Puzzles, David Wells, Penguin, 1992

Mathematical Puzzling, A Gardiner, Oxford, 1987

Pentagames, Books UK Ltd, 1993

Points of Departure 1,2,3,4; Primary Points of Departure, ATM, 1990 onwards

Lighting Mathematical Fires, Derek Holton & Charles Lovitt, Curriculum Corporation, 1998 (Australia)

Getting Started, Jim Smith, The Mathematical Association, 1999

Learning and Teaching Mathematics Without a Textbook, Mike Ollerton, ATM, 2002

Mathematics From Around The World, Phil Dodd, published by the author, 1992

People Maths, Alan Bloomfield, Stanley Thornes, 1990